The Secret Life of the Underwear Champ

Betty Miles is the author of over twenty books for children including, *The Real Me, All It Takes Is Practice, The Trouble With Thirteen* and recently, *Maudie and Me and the Dirty Book* (all Knopf)).

A graduate of Antioch College, Ms. Miles is on the editorial board of *Children's Literature in Education*. She has been associate editor of the Bank Street Readers and taught children's literature at Bank Street College of Education for many years.

Ms. Miles lives in Rockland County, New York, with her husband. They have three grown children.

The
Secret Life
of the
Underwear
Champ

by BETTY MILES
illustrated by Dan Jones

ALFRED A. KNOPF · NEW YORK

This is a Borzoi Book
Published by Alfred A. Knopf, Inc.

Copyright © 1981 by Betty Miles
Illustrations Copyright © 1981 by Dan Jones
All rights reserved under International and Pan-American
Copyright Conventions. Published in the United States by
Alfred A. Knopf, Inc., New York, and simultaneously in
Canada by Random House of Canada Limited, Toronto.
Distributed by Random House, Inc., New York.
Manufactured in the United States of America.
10 9 8 7 6

Library of Congress Cataloging in Publication Data
Miles, Betty.
The secret life of the
underwear champ. (Capers)
Summary: Ten-year-old Larry is "discovered" on
the street and asked to appear in a television
commercial. Only later does he find out what he is
advertising. [1. Television advertising—Fiction]
I. Title. II. Series.
PZ7.M594Se 1981 [Fic] 80-15651
ISBN 0-394-84563-3 (pbk.)
ISBN 0-394-94563-8 (lib. bdg.)

*For Saul and
Benjamin Fussiner*

Contents

The Secret Life of the Underwear Champ

1

I Am Discovered

The whole thing began on a street corner in New York City. I was standing there innocently with Mom, waiting for a bus.

We don't even live in New York. We live in Hazelton, Connecticut, which is about an hour away by train. We'd come in to see this New York dentist we go to because he's a cousin of Mom's. I don't like him. He's the kind of man who calls you Sonny. My name's Larry.

The dentist poked around in my mouth till he found a cavity, and then he filled it. Afterwards, we had to take the crosstown bus to Grand Central Station. We were waiting for it at the stop in front of his office. My mouth was numb from the Novocaine.

The new filling felt gigantic. I wondered if the dentist could have made some mistake. I wished the stupid bus would come before I froze to death standing there. A cold wind was blowing, and all I had on was my baseball jacket and cap.

It had been warm back in Hazelton when we started out. Back home, Robert and the other kids had probably been playing ball all afternoon.

All of a sudden, a big gust of wind came along and blew my hat off my head—the official Yankees baseball cap I got at a game last summer! I started to run after it. If I lost my good hat, or a car ran over it, that would be the last straw. The hat bounced along the sidewalk ahead of me. Just before it blew off the curb, I put out my foot and stopped it.

"That's *him!*" someone yelled, as I bent down.

I looked up. A man and a woman were running across the street. The woman was pointing at me. As casually as I could, I wiped off my hat and put it back on.

"That's the boy!" the man agreed, as they headed toward me.

I turned around. There wasn't any other boy in back of me. Nervously, I started edging over to Mom.

"Wait!" the woman called frantically. "You, with the red hair—stop!"

My hair's red. She had to mean me. What had *I* done? I had never even seen these people before. Trying to be cool, I pulled my hat down and backed away faster.

Mom ran up and grabbed my arm protectively. "What's going on?" she asked.

We stood close together as the couple rushed up to us. They looked sort of like grandparents. I wondered if this was a new thing in New York City—people dressing up to look like grandparents and then kidnapping you.

"Such a good-looking boy!" the woman said, beaming. She looked me up and down the way a grandmother, or a lady pretending to be one, would. She had a stiff black hairdo that might have been a wig.

6

Mom squeezed my arm tighter. "Yes," she said in a strained voice.

I didn't say anything. The Novocaine was wearing off. My tooth began to ache. The people were practically standing on top of us.

The woman leaned across me and grabbed Mom's coat collar. "We are the Zigmunds!" she said dramatically.

Was that some kind of gang name? I took a step back.

"From the Zigmund Agency." The man stepped after me and grabbed *my* collar. "We need this boy!" he said. He reached into his coat, took out a card, and gave it to Mom.

Mom read the card. Then she laughed in a relieved way. "Oh! You're from the Zigmund *Model* Agency?"

"We are," the woman said, patting my shoulder as though I were a little dog. "And this boy is the answer to our prayers!"

Then, while I stood there squeezed in between them, the Zigmunds began this long story about how they had been hunting all over for a redheaded boy like me because they needed one for a commercial they were making.

The Zigmunds talked so fast and so loud that I couldn't take in all the details. But I got the main idea.

They wanted me to be on *television!*

2
Me, a Star?

I couldn't believe it.

"Who, *me?*" I gulped.

Mom pressed my back to make me stand straight. "Well," she said, sounding excited. "*I* think he's a good-looking boy. But then of course I'm prejudiced."

"No, no, he's adorable!" Mrs. Zigmund lifted up my cap and tweaked my hair. "Just look at those curls!"

I ducked. I hate it when people mention my curls.

"*Terrific* curls!" Mr. Zigmund boomed out. "And freckles! They'll go crazy for the freckles!" He thumped my back. "A great little all-around guy, this fella," he said. "I bet he's a real athlete, too. Am I right, son?"

"Yeah." I *am* a pretty good athlete, actually. Especially in baseball. I wondered how he knew. Maybe from the quick way I had fielded my cap.

"He does very well in school, too," Mom added. She always has to get that in.

"I knew it!" shouted Mr. Zigmund triumphantly. "A regular all-around boy. What did I tell you?" He thumped my back again. He was a short fat man with a round pink face and a bald head. He looked sort of like a middle-aged baby.

Mrs. Zigmund bent over me as though I were a little kid. "What do you say, honey?" she asked. I could smell her perfume. She had a bright red mouth and big round glasses. "Will you come and see us at our office, with Mommy?"

For a second I thought she meant *her* Mommy. Then I realized she was talking about Mom.

"I don't know," I said, uncomfortably. I looked out over Mrs. Zigmund's shoulder. "Mom—the bus is coming!"

Mom started into the street, waving it

down. "We have a train to catch at Grand Central," she explained.

But Mr. Zigmund pulled her back and dashed into the street himself. "Taxi! Taxi!" he shouted.

The bus rolled on and a taxi drew up in front of us with a screech. Mr. Zigmund pushed Mom and me inside. Mrs. Zigmund climbed in after us, nearly squashing me as she settled onto the seat.

"Grand Central Station," Mr. Zigmund told the driver as he got in the other side. He leaned forward seriously. "Can't let you get away!" he said. "Not before you promise to bring this fella in to see us, Mrs. ——?"

"Pryor," Mom said. "And this is Larry." She poked me so I'd stick my hand out.

"Wonderful!" Mr. Zigmund reached over to me and pumped my hand up and down. "Pleased to meet you, Larry!" Then he grabbed Mom's hand and pumped *it*, beaming, as the taxi bumped along the street.

I wriggled out from under Mrs. Zigmund and leaned back against the seat. It was nice and warm in the taxi. Mom and I don't usually take cabs because they cost too much. I still couldn't believe what was happening. For a second, I wondered if the Zigmunds were the kind of kidnappers who carried kids off in taxis. How would we get in touch with Dad and my sister?

But the Zigmunds were talking fast about their agency. They couldn't be making it all up. They said it was the biggest agency in the city. Everybody in advertising wanted

Zigmund models for their commercials.

"We have them in every age, shape, color, size," Mr. Zigmund said. "You need a grandmother, we supply a grandmother. You need a plumber, we've got him, tools and all. Your college professor types, bride types—"

"Babies!" interrupted Mrs. Zigmund. "Children!" She poked me in the side, smiling confidentially. "You're a lucky boy. You're going to get to meet Suzanne *Ridley!*"

"Who's she?" I asked.

Mrs. Zigmund gasped. "You watch television, and you're asking me who's *she?*" She put her hand on her chest. "Suzanne Ridley," she said, "simply happens to be the most famous, the cutest, the most talented little girl—"

"Is she that little girl in the Purr-fection Cat Food commercials?" Mom asked.

Oh, her! I'd seen those ads. The girl in them was stupid.

"That's Suzanne!" Mr. Zigmund said eagerly. "The hottest little model in TV today. Cat food, dog food, yogurt—you name it, she's in it. And she's making big money for her family, let me tell you." He looked significantly at Mom.

"I suppose she must be," Mom said thoughtfully.

I wondered how big "big money" was. It would probably be big enough to buy a ten-speed bike. I wondered if Suzanne Ridley owned one.

The taxi turned onto the ramp by Grand Central.

"Now, here's the deal, Mrs. Pryor." Mr. Zigmund began talking faster. "I'm not making any promises, but I want to shoot a test tape on Larry here, and show it to the ChampWin Knitting Mills people. They have a contract with us for a big new advertising campaign—maybe four, five commercials. The theme's family fitness. The idea is to show a family wearing Champ-Win products while they keep fit. A red-haired family. We've got a Mother and a Father, we've got Suzanne for Sister—" He broke off and patted my head. "And now, with Larry here, I think we've found Brother. Red hair freckles, athletic, eight or nine years old—"

"I'm *ten*," I interrupted. You would think he could have seen that.

"Nine, ten, what's the difference?" said Mr. Zigmund quickly, as the taxi pulled up at the entrance to the station. "ChampWin Knitting Mills isn't asking for his birth certificate. Now then!" He pulled a date book out of his pocket. "You'll bring Larry to see us—how about next Monday?"

Mom hesitated. "Of course, we'd have to talk all this over at home—"

The taxi driver reached back to open the door on Mom's side.

"Monday at four-thirty," said Mr. Zigmund. "It's a great opportunity, believe me, Mrs. Pryor." He thumped my knee. "Right, Larry? What do you say, fella?"

I didn't know what to say. The taxi behind us was honking. In a way, it might be sort of exciting. If I was on TV, everybody would see me. Robert. All the kids. People I didn't even know. I could be famous!

Mom and the Zigmunds were looking at me expectantly.

"Well, sure, I guess," I said.

"Wonderful!" said Mrs. Zigmund, pinching my cheek.

"You aren't going to be sorry, I promise you," said Mr. Zigmund.

He was wrong.

3

Complications

The minute we got home, my sister started in.

"Why would anyone want *Larry* on TV?" she asked.

She was probably jealous. Nancy thinks she's so great, just because she's a teenager. She's always standing in front of mirrors admiring herself. Maybe she wished someone had seen *her* on the street and asked her to be on TV. Anyway, she made me feel stupid.

But Dad was different. "How *about* that?" he said, squeezing my shoulder. "So you're going to be a television star!" He smiled at Mom. "This family might be on easy street after all, if Larry gets onto a good thing.

How much do you think they pay those kids in commercials?"

He and Mom are always worried about money. Dad's in the construction business, and he was laid off a lot last winter because of bad weather. Mom works part time as a bookkeeper in an auto repair shop. She doesn't make very much.

"I don't know," she said to Dad. "Probably lots, when they're famous. But for a new face—"

"For a face like Larry's," Nancy put in quickly, "two cents an hour would be about right. *If* he washed it."

"Come on, Nance," Dad said. "Don't knock it." He looked serious. "We could use the money."

Nancy looked embarrassed, but she kept on. "I can think of better ways to get it," she mumbled, "than making a fool of yourself on TV in front of the whole entire world."

As soon as she said that, I began to worry. The kids I know always laugh at stupid commercials. It would be horrible if I was in one and they laughed at *me*.

18

"Maybe I shouldn't do it," I said. "I mean, I don't know *how* to be on television."

"Oh, you'd learn," said Mom, giving Nancy a look. "That wouldn't be a problem. What I don't know," she said to Dad, "is how I'll manage it, getting Larry to the city for appointments." She set down her coffee cup. "I could probably take some afternoons off, if I went in earlier in the mornings. But I don't know how often I could arrange that."

"Nancy could help out," Dad said. "She could start supper when she gets home from school."

Nancy made a face. For some reason, I felt a little sorry for her.

"Listen, Nancy," I said. "If I got rich or something, you'd be rich, too. You could buy stuff."

Nancy smiled at me. "Hey, that's sweet, Larry. No kidding." She patted my hand. "And I could tell my friends that the cute boy in the ChampWin commercials is my brother."

Now she was trying to be nice, but that just made me more uncomfortable. I didn't want her to go around saying how cute I was. Cute is disgusting. Right then, I definitely decided I wouldn't say a word about this yet to Robert. After all, I didn't even know for sure that it would happen.

Still, a couple of times that weekend I nearly came out with it, just to see his reaction. But I kept my mouth shut. I didn't want Robert making any jokes until I knew more.

Then on Monday, the day Mom was taking me to see the Zigmunds, something else came up to complicate everything. Coach Bryant announced baseball tryouts.

Our school team, the Cardinals, is in this league with teams from the other schools in Hazelton. Last year, the Milton Blue Jays won the championship. This year everyone thinks the Cardinals could win. That's why I was really hoping to make the team.

Robert's the only kid in our class who made it last year, when we were fourth graders. He's a terrific pitcher. But this year we were the top grade in school, so it was logical that a lot of us would make the team.

I was pretty sure I would. Not to boast or anything, but I'm a fairly good player. I may be small, but I'm fast.

Still, I couldn't count on just automatically getting picked. There were a lot of good players in our class. So when Coach Bryant brought up the tryouts, I started worrying. First, about making the team at all, and second, about what would happen if I did but then I had to go to the city for a commercial on a day we had practice, or a game.

"I've scheduled tryouts for Wednesday, after school," the coach said. "Let's see hands. How many of you are planning to come out?"

A lot of hands went up, maybe twelve or thirteen. Steve Knudson was waving his in the air. He thinks he's a pretty hot player. He's okay. It's just that he's so bossy. And he always tries to grab first base, which is my best position. Knudson may be taller, but so what? I couldn't help wishing that he wouldn't make the team at all.

"The first league game is just three weeks

from now," Coach Bryant said. "It's going to take a lot of practice to get a team in shape. I don't want anybody showing up for tryouts unless they're ready to practice three, four afternoons a week, right up to the first game. Is that clear?"

Everyone except me yelled "Yes!"

I poked Robert. "What if you had to *do* something one of those days?"

"Oh, the coach would let you off if you had a good excuse," Robert said. "He just wants people to know he's serious about practice. A couple of times last year he blew up when someone missed practice two days in a row."

"Well, sure," I said. "I can see how that would bother him." I was thinking fast. I could probably make the Wednesday tryouts. The Zigmunds wouldn't have work for me that soon, even if they signed me up today. But what about all the other practices? And the games? I wondered if I should say something to Coach Bryant now. But then, why bring it up before I knew anything? If I told the coach, he might not want me on the team at all.

"I was just thinking, what if I had to go to the dentist on practice days," I told Robert.

He looked surprised. "You just *went* to the dentist."

"Yeah." I felt trapped. "But see, there was this one thing he didn't completely finish." I opened my mouth and pointed vaguely toward the back.

Robert didn't bother to look. "Relax," he said. "If you have to go to the dentist, the coach'll let you." He nudged me. "Look who has her hand up—old Stockton. I feel sorry for the Cardinals if *she* makes the team."

Betsy Stockton lives on Robert's block. She's always hanging around after school, wanting to walk home with him. But Robert doesn't like her to. At least, he says he doesn't. I don't know. I think maybe Betsy's his girl friend. Stuff like that is hard to tell, but you can guess. Robert's always making jokes about Stockton and grabbing her lunch bag or pulling her hair.

"I bet you wouldn't mind if she made the team," I said, just to see what he'd answer.

He made a face. "Oh, yes I would," he said quickly. He looked sort of embarrassed, so I decided I'd better lay off.

We have lunch period after gym. In the cafeteria, everybody was talking about try-outs and guessing who the coach would pick for the team. A lot of kids said he'd pick me. I wasn't so sure. Anyway, it looked as though the Zigmunds had picked me first. I felt funny thinking about what I had to do after school, and not saying anything to Robert. Boy, would he be surprised if he knew!

John Wyatt came up to us in the lunch line. "Want to get together this afternoon for some batting practice?" he asked.

"Sure," Robert said.

"I can't," I had to say.

Robert looked at me, surprised. "How come?"

"I have to go to New York," I said uncomfortably. "To the dentist."

"What *is* this with the dentist, all of a

sudden?" Robert asked impatiently. "You didn't say you had to go *today.*"

"I just remembered," I mumbled uncomfortably. "See, the dentist told me two different days I could come. And I just now remembered that Mom picked this day instead of the other one."

I hate making up excuses. It makes you feel like a dope. But I could see that from now on I was going to have to make up a lot of them.

4

Meeting Famous Suzanne

The Zigmund Agency was on Forty-ninth
Street, a few blocks from Grand Central. I
stuck close to Mom as we crossed the streets
in crowds of people. Everybody seemed to
be in a hurry. I didn't see any other kids
around. I felt like a freak.

I looked at the street signs as we walked
along, trying to memorize the way in case I
had to come by myself some day. Hansel
and Gretel would have had a tough time
finding their way in New York City. If you
threw any pieces of bread down on Madison
Avenue, the pigeons would eat them right
up. You wouldn't have a chance to follow
them back.

We found the Zigmunds' building and

walked across the lobby, which was as big as a church. Then Mom and I squeezed into an elevator between two women with suitcase-sized handbags and a man holding a tray of take-out coffee. People got on and off at every floor. They all seemed to know each other. I wondered if they could guess where we were going. I hoped Mom wasn't going to tell them.

The elevator stopped at the sixteenth floor, and Mom pushed me out. We crossed the hall toward some big glass doors with ZIGMUND MODEL AGENCY written across them in gold letters. Inside, a woman at a giant desk stared out at us. Mom opened the door and nudged me through ahead of her.

The woman behind the desk looked up crossly, as though we were interrupting her. "Your name?"

"Pryor," Mom said. "This is Larry Pryor." She said it as though I were already famous. "We have an appointment with Mr. and Mrs. Zigmund." Before she could fix my collar or something, I headed over to one of the big couches in front of the windows. I practically sank down to the floor when I sat on it, it was so soft.

Mom came toward me, taking a comb from her purse.

"Mom!" I said, ducking.

"Now, Larry," she whispered. "Don't get excited."

She was the one who was acting excited. I just felt numb.

"You're going to be fine," Mom went on, patting my hair down. "Remember—they just want you to act natural."

The trouble was, I didn't *feel* natural. I'd never seen a place like the Zigmunds' waiting room before, except maybe in the movies. It was huge. They had plants as big as trees all over the place. There was a giant glass table in front of us with about a hundred magazines on it. The walls were covered with advertisements in silver frames.

Suddenly a door opened and Mrs. Zigmund rushed across the room.

"Larry!" she said, kissing my cheek with a smack. "Here you *are!*" She pinched my arm as though she needed to prove it.

"Guess who's here," she went on excitedly. "Mr. Ron Corman, the president of ChampWin Knitting Mills! We've been telling him all about the darling little boy we found on the street."

She made it sound as though I'd been an abandoned baby or something.

"We're going to put Larry in front of the cameras right away," Mrs. Zigmund said to Mom. "Then we'll bring Mr. Corman in to meet him and look at his tape."

In front of the cameras! Suddenly I wished I could go home. What was I doing here?

"Ready?" Mrs. Zigmund held out her hand.

Behind her, Mom was signaling me to stand up. I did, without taking Mrs. Zigmund's hand. It was hard to get out of that couch, it was so deep. I knocked a couple of magazines off the table as I got up and followed Mom and Mrs. Zigmund across the room.

"And you'll never guess who *else* is here," Mrs. Zigmund burbled, leading us down a hall, around a corner, and up to a door that said STUDIO—QUIET, PLEASE.

"Who?" I asked stupidly.

Mrs. Zigmund opened the door dramatically and pushed us into a big room with some chairs in the back. The other end of the room was all lit up, like a stage. A bunch of people were standing there, surrounded by cameras and lights on tripods and a bunch of TV sets. A familiar-looking girl with short red hair sat behind a table, facing the cameras.

Mom stared at her. "Is that—"

"Suzanne *Ridley!*" Mrs. Zigmund said triumphantly. "Isn't that wonderful? Suzanne's here to be in Larry's test and to meet Mr. Corman." She patted my head. "We knew you'd like to have a little friend your own age to talk to."

A little friend! Suzanne Ridley was a *star*. She probably would be too stuck-up to say anything. I stared at her. No wonder she looked familiar. I must have seen her in a million commercials.

Mrs. Zigmund pulled a chair over to Mom. "Now, Mrs. Pryor, you just sit down right here, and I'll take Larry up to meet Suzanne."

"Mom—" I said weakly. I didn't *want* to meet Suzanne. I didn't want to sit up there at the table with her, in front of all those people. In front of the *cameras*. I wanted to go home.

Mrs. Zigmund was dragging me toward the stage. "Here we are!" she called in a loud voice as I stumbled after her. "Here's Larry!"

Everybody turned to look at me. Suzanne stared out coolly from behind the table.

Mrs. Zigmund practically shoved me in front of it. "Suzanne, sweetie," she said.

31

"This is Larry, the wonderful little boy I've been telling you about."

Suzanne looked me over. "Hi," she said.

"Hi," I said. I tried to smile casually, but my mouth was stiff.

"I won't introduce the whole crew now," said Mrs. Zigmund. "We want to start right in. But this is Bud Slater, our director." She pointed to a tall man with a moustache. "Bud, this is little Larry Pryor."

Why did she have to keep saying *little?* She made me feel like a midget.

Bud Slater stuck out his hand and shook mine. "Pleased to meet you," he said, as though he actually was.

"Yeah," I said. I felt like a dope with everybody looking me over. Especially Suzanne. I wished she wouldn't stare that way.

"Okay, Larry," Bud said. "Just sit right down next to Suzanne and we'll get started." He laughed as I hesitated. "Don't worry. This isn't going to hurt a bit."

I wondered if he was making fun of me.

A woman fastened a little mike, the kind newscasters wear, around my neck. People began pushing cameras around and bringing lights over to the table.

Mrs. Zigmund gave me a little shove. "Sit down and get acquainted, dear," she said. "I'm going back to sit with Mommy."

This time I knew she meant *my* mother, not hers, but it still seemed a dumb thing to call her. Awkwardly, I walked around the table and pulled out the chair next to Suzanne, bumping my leg on it. The bright lights glared into my eyes so I could hardly see.

"You going to be in the ChampWin commercials?" Suzanne asked right away.

"I don't know." I blinked. "I guess so. If I do okay now."

"Oh, any stupe can do this," Suzanne said quickly.

I wondered if she meant *I* was stupid, or what.

"Anyway, our hair's about the same," she went on. "That's really all they care about. Look." She pointed over to the side.

I looked where she was pointing and just about jumped out of my chair. There was this big color picture of the two of us on a giant TV!

"How did they do *that?*" I asked, staring at the picture of myself asking it. I shifted nervously in my chair. The picture of me shifted, too.

"Oh, that's just a studio monitor," Suzanne said casually. "It shows whatever the camera takes. The camera that's on."

I looked at the cameras. There were three of them. "Which one's on?"

"The one with the red light lit up," Suzanne said, studying the monitor matter-of-factly. She didn't seem at all nervous.

"Okay, kids," said Bud Slater. "We've turned on the mikes, and the tape's rolling. Let's hear you say something, Larry."

I choked up. My hands were sweating. I couldn't think of anything to say.

"Where do you live?" Suzanne asked.

"In Con—" I heard my voice squeak out. I cleared my throat. "In Connecticut. Where do you?"

"In New Jersey. What grade are you in?"

"Fifth." I started to scratch my nose but I pulled my hand back when I saw it on the monitor.

"Me, too," Suzanne said. "Are you ten?"

"Yeah." What *was* this, some kind of interview?

"So'm I." Suzanne giggled. "So that's funny, that we're supposed to be a brother and sister in the commercial. How *could* we be, unless we were twins?"

"I don't know," I said. She had a point. Maybe that would be a reason to get me out of this.

Suzanne stuck out her hand above my head. "I guess I could be your *older* sister," she said. "I'm about two inches taller than you."

"Yeah." Boy! She seemed to think she was hot stuff because she was taller. How could she tell for sure, anyway, with us sitting down? She sort of reminded me of Nancy.

Except Nancy wasn't on TV.

"Have you been in a lot of commercials?" I asked, just to make conversation. I wasn't that interested, but I had to say something, with the cameras zooming in on me.

"Oh, sure." Suzanne started to recite. "Cat food, dog food, cameras, life insurance —" She broke off. "I worked with this really dumb boy on the life insurance commercial. He kept forgetting his lines."

"Oh." I hadn't thought about *lines*. I wondered if they expected you to memorize lots of stuff. I'm not so good at memorizing. About the only thing I know by heart is a poem called "Welcome, Pussy Willow," from first grade.

"Okay—cut!" Bob Slater called. The monitor suddenly went blank. "Set the tape up so we can run it for Mr. Corman," he said to a man behind him. "You looked great, Larry," he told me. "What did *you* think, Mrs. Zigmund?" he called to her.

"Wonderful!" she shouted back. "I'm going to get Mr. Corman in here to see the tape." She ran out of the room.

I looked up and saw Mom beaming at me.

"Is that your mother?" Suzanne asked.

"Yeah." I was embarrassed. I didn't want her to think my mother always had to bring me places.

"I come in by myself," Suzanne said. She was twisting a curl of hair around her finger. It was almost exactly the same color as mine. "I bet you don't even know what the commercials are going to be *for*," she added mysteriously.

"For clothes, I thought," I told her. "T-shirts and stuff. Isn't that what Champ-Win Mills makes?"

"Yeah, but that's not all." Suzanne giggled. "They also just happen to make *underwear!*" She waited expectantly for my reaction.

"They *do?*" I squeaked out.

"Yeah. And the commercials are supposed to show this family doing different sports in their ChampWin underwear!"

I gulped. "How would they show *that?* Take X-rays through their clothes, or what?" *I* couldn't believe it.

Suzanne giggled again. "I don't know. We might not even *wear* clothes, I guess, except for the underwear."

"Oh," I said weakly, pushing my chair back. I didn't want to act shocked, but I was. How could I be on TV in my underwear? What if somebody *saw* me? I looked back at Mom, wishing she'd get up and take me out of here. But she was still smiling proudly at me. I wondered what she'd say when she found out.

Just then Mrs. Zigmund came back with Mr. Zigmund and another man.

"Hel*lo*, Larry!" Mr. Zigmund boomed out, heading for me. "I hear you looked terrific!"

I couldn't answer. I was thinking of all the people who might see me on television in my underwear. Robert, and the other kids at school. The neighbors. My parents' friends. My teachers! I would just about pass out if I thought Ms. Sanford or Coach Bryant were looking at me.

Mr. Zigmund turned to the other man. "This is Larry Pryor, Ron, the new find we've been telling you about. Larry, this is Ron Corman, the president of ChampWin Knitting Mills." The way he said it, you would have thought Mr. Corman was the President of the United States.

I stood up awkwardly to shake Mr. Corman's hand. He looked me up and down.

"Small for his age, isn't he?" he said. "I was expecting a more athletic-looking kid.

A little more husky."

"Oh, Larry's a big athlete," said Mr. Zigmund quickly. "Aren't you, fella? Tell Mr. Corman."

"I guess so," I said, almost too numb by now to be insulted.

"Well, let's have a look at the tape," Mr. Corman said.

So Bud put the tape on the playback machine and everybody gathered around the monitor to watch.

In a way, it was pretty exciting to see myself on a TV screen. I didn't look that bad, actually, except for the way I kept ducking my head when I talked. But otherwise, I was all right. Everybody said so, including Suzanne. Mrs. Zigmund said I was wonderful. Even Mr. Corman seemed to think I was okay. For a second, I let myself think about getting famous.

Then, behind me, I heard Mrs. Zigmund asking Mom what size I took in underclothes, and the whole horrible situation really dawned on me. I was going to be famous for being on TV in my underwear!

5

Underwear Everywhere?

Two days later we had baseball tryouts, and I made the team.

Any other time, I would have been all excited. But now, a lot of the pleasure was out of it. Getting on the Cardinals just made my life more complicated.

Right away, Coach Bryant handed out practice schedules. Practically every school afternoon was filled in except for teachers' meeting days. I didn't know how I was going to get out of practice without explaining everything to the coach. But I didn't *want* to explain. If I told him that I couldn't come to all the practice sessions, he might not let me stay on the team. That was one problem.

And then, on top of that, there was the

whole problem of underwear. That was what *really* bothered me.

Most people probably never notice how often underwear comes up in life. I know I never did before. But now I couldn't stop thinking about it. There was always something to remind me. Like putting underwear on in the morning and taking it off at night. Throwing it in the wash, and putting it away again in the drawer. Seeing packs of it in the supermarket and piles of it in the dime store. It was always there.

The thing is, everybody wears underwear, no matter who they are, or where they live. No matter how famous they are, too— even the *President* wears it. I thought of that when I saw him on the television news one night. The minute he came on, I started wondering if he was wearing ChampWin underwear. What a commercial that would make!

But the thing is that even though everybody wears underwear, nobody wants to talk about it. It's an embarrassing topic. Like, in first or second grade, practically the worst thing you could say to another kid was "I see London, I see France, I see So-and-so's *underpants.*" Robert and I used to tease Betsy Stockton that way when we were little. She'd get furious.

When we were older, a couple of times Robert and I took the Sears catalogue down to his game room and snickered at the underwear ads in it, especially the girls'. And one time in school, I think it was just last year, Kevin Halloran's jeans ripped across the seat when he bent over, and our whole class practically had a fit because we could see his white underpants sticking through. We kidded Halloran about it for weeks. Now, when it was too late, I wished we hadn't given him such a hard time. I mean, what was so funny?

That's what I said to Nancy when Mom told her what the ChampWin commercials would be about and she broke up.

"What's so funny about *that?*" I asked.

"Nothing," Nancy said, quickly, still laughing.

"Nancy!" Mom glanced at me. "Don't be

childish, honey. It's nothing to laugh about. From what Mrs. Zigmund said, this commercial could mean the start of a big career for Larry. A whole series of ads, and on national television. Just think of the exposure!"

That's exactly what I was worried about— the exposure.

"Anyway, it might not happen," I said. "Mr. Corman could still change his mind." Something *might* go wrong. The Zigmunds' building could get struck by lightning, or the ChampWin company could go bankrupt, or something.

"That's true," Dad said seriously. "I think we should just keep this to ourselves until it's definite." He smiled at me. "If everything works out, the money Larry earns could be a big help. But we don't want to get our hopes up. Then we won't be disappointed."

"Yeah," I said, feeling guilty. It *would* be good to help my family out. That was the one side. But I couldn't stop hoping it wouldn't happen. Then I wouldn't have to make up excuses for the coach, or explain everything to Robert. I wouldn't have to worry about the embarrassment. As much as I wanted a new ten-speed bike, I would have given up the idea of it forever right then, just to get out of making an underwear commercial. My old bike was okay. My old *life* was okay. I hated to think what my new one might be like.

6

The Worst Happens!

The day of the first Cardinals practice started badly and ended worse.

Steve Knudson came over as soon as I walked into Ms. Sanford's room that morning.

"What position you going out for, Pryor?" he asked, in this sort of sarcastic tone. I wondered if he'd been talking to Robert or to Betsy Stockton. I'd told both of them I might try out for first.

"I don't know," I said, not wanting to tell him. Coach Bryant hadn't assigned our positions yet. He said we'd switch around for a few practices so he could see how we did at different places. "It's up to the coach," I said.

"I thought you were going to try for first base," Stockton said, coming up behind me. Robert was with her.

"Yeah," he began. "You said—"

"I don't care what I play," I said, feeling trapped. "*Maybe* I'll try for first."

"Oh, yeah?" Knudson poked me so hard it hurt. "I wouldn't count on it, if I were you."

"How come?" I could guess.

"It takes a big guy to hold down first," Knudson said with a self-satisfied smirk.

"You gotta have reach in that position." He's the biggest kid in our class. That's probably why he always thinks he's so great.

Ms. Sanford hurried in. "Morning, kids. Get yourselves settled. We have a lot to do this morning. Our papers are here." She started handing out the weekly newspapers we subscribe to. "There's an interesting article on page one," she said. "About television commercials."

I jumped.

"I want you to read it carefully," she went on. "Then we'll discuss it together."

Robert turned around in his seat, pointing at my paper. "Look—a picture of Choc-O-Mars!" He once ate four of them in a row when I was over at his house. Then he threw up. Afterwards, we made up an advertisement: "Eat 'em up, Throw 'em up, Choc-O-Mars!"

"Turn around, Robert," Ms. Sanford said. "Start reading the article, please."

I bent over my paper and tried to concentrate. I could feel my ears turning red as I skimmed through the article. It was all about the bad influence of TV commercials! Why did Ms. Sanford have to pick that topic today? I didn't want to sit there while everybody discussed it. What would I say? I tried to pay attention to the article. At least, it wasn't about *all* commercials—just the ones for junk food. I wouldn't make one of them. I would never take money for telling little kids that junk food was good. At least underwear doesn't rot your teeth.

Naturally, Knudson was the first one to speak. "Everybody knows that commercials are untrue," he said. "Anyway, most kids just laugh at them."

Oh, man. If he saw me in mine, he'd probably be hysterical.

I kept my eyes on my paper as the discussion went on. Everybody had some disgusting commercial to tell about. It was awful.

Finally, Ms. Sanford changed the subject from commercials to the basic foods for good nutrition, and then pretty soon it was time for math. As soon as we got into fractions I felt better.

But all day the underwear commercial was on my mind. Sooner or later, the kids would find out. I couldn't keep it a secret forever. The whole school was going to make fun of me!

By the end of the day I was a nervous wreck. It was a lousy way to feel before our first practice. I ran out onto the field with the others, hoping I wouldn't drop the first ball someone threw to me.

"Okay, guys!" Robert yelled as we spread out.

Knudson headed for first base before I could get there, so I went over to shortstop. Robert began pitching to Peggy Armbruster, who everyone calls Arm*bruiser* because she can hit so hard. Peggy lined one into left field and made it to second before Halloran retrieved the ball.

"Hang in there, Robert!" I shouted.

Stockton came up next and got a single. Then a fourth-grade kid I didn't know who was on the team hit a high pop fly. I saw it floating slowly through the air toward me. I raced back, reached out my arm, and caught

it—right in the center of my glove. Man, I did it!

"All *right*, Pryor!" yelled Robert.

"Nice fielding there," Coach Bryant called from the sidelines.

I felt really good after the catch. Maybe, if I could keep on performing like that, the coach would want me to play short. I decided that would be okay. In a way, it's even more crucial than first. I slapped my fist into my glove.

"Come on, guys!" I yelled, squatting down to be ready for the next pitch.

Just then, a little kid came out of the building and trotted over to Coach Bryant. The coach bent down to him.

"Pryor!" he yelled, straightening up. "Phone call for you in the office!"

Oh, man—not *now!* Disgustedly, I threw my glove down. Then I picked it back up, walked off the field, and headed for the building. I could feel everyone's eyes on me, but I didn't turn around.

Even before I got inside, I knew what was coming.

Half an hour later, I was on the train to New York City.

7

Alone in the Big Apple

And I was alone.

Mom had sounded frantic on the phone. It seems that Mrs. Zigmund had tracked her down at work and asked her to rush me into the city. It was an emergency. Mr. Corman had learned that some other company was bringing out a line of sports underwear. To beat the competition, he wanted the first commercial made *fast*. The Zigmunds were rounding up a camera crew and calling all the actors. They wanted me to be at their office by four o'clock.

"But I'm in the middle of practice!" I said. "What'll I tell the coach?"

"There's no time to tell him anything," Mom said hurriedly. "You'll have to rush just to make the train. I'll write him a note to explain everything." She hesitated. "The problem is, I just don't see how I can come with you, Larry. The auditor's here—"

The auditor is a big thing at Mom's job. He only comes about every three months, to check the books.

"It's okay," I said quickly. "I can go by myself." I wondered if I really could.

"Remember how we did it before?" Mom asked. "We turned right when we went out of the station, and then we walked two blocks up Madison Avenue."

"Sure." What I remembered was the traffic, and the crowds. I wondered what I'd do if I got lost or something.

"If you get lost, you could always call me at work," Mom said quickly.

"Mom! I'm not going to get *lost!*" I was so upset I practically yelled at her. Then I felt embarrassed because of the school secretary.

"I'm sure you'll be fine," Mom said uncertainly. "Remember, don't talk to strangers. And turn right outside Grand

Central. The Zigmunds will take you back there afterwards, so you don't have to worry about that part. Oh, and the secretary said she'd lend you money for the train." She paused. "You'll be fine," she repeated.

"Yeah," I said.

"Have a good time, hon," Mom said. "Goodbye!" She made a kiss noise into the phone.

I hung up fast, hoping the secretary hadn't heard *that*.

She smiled, handing me a ten-dollar bill.

"Your mother asked me to lend you this," she said. "Going to the city all by yourself, are you?"

"Yeah." I hoped she didn't guess it was my first time.

I hurried downstairs to the empty locker room and changed my clothes, trying not to listen to the shouts from the field. Then I sprinted the three blocks down Erie Street to the train station. The crossing light was flashing when I got there. The train came clanging in and I climbed on, ducking into the first car. There was nobody in it.

I sank into a seat and caught my breath as the train jerked and started up. At the first crossing I leaned forward to look out of the window. There was my school—and there, spread out on the diamond like players on a television screen, was my team!

"Way to go, guys," I said silently, watching them until the field disappeared. I wondered what they'd said about me after I left. I wondered what they were *going* to say, when they found out what I was doing!

The door clanked open, and the conductor came into the car. Bracing himself against my seat, he pulled out a roll of tickets.

"Round trip to New York," I said casually.

"Going to the Big Apple by yourself, eh?" He punched a ticket and handed it to me with my change. Then he patted my head as though I were some little kid and swung on past. The car door slammed closed behind him, and I was alone again.

I watched the swampy fields of marsh grass go by without really seeing them. My stomach was jumping along in time with the train wheels. I tried to imagine what making the commercial would be like. Suzanne was lucky to be so experienced. I wondered if they would give me a long speech to learn. Oh, man!

The marshes finally gave way to factories and apartment buildings. We were getting nearer to the city. I tried to picture the walk from the station to the Zigmunds' office, but I couldn't see it clearly in my mind. I leaned back and tried to relax. The ride seemed to be taking an awfully long time. I hoped the train wasn't going to be late.

After a while there was nothing but rows of high-rise buildings outside the window. The train shuddered to a stop for a second, lurched up again, and headed into a tunnel. Then the car lights flickered and the windows went dark. I got up and walked to the door so I'd be ready to jump out as soon as the train stopped. I had to get to the Zigmunds' office on time!

There was a sudden sharp screech of wheels that threw me against the door. "Grand Central!" a voice shouted. "All out!"

I followed the crowds down the platform and into the station, heading for the information booth. Mom always said we should meet there if we got separated. It felt funny to *be* separated. The clock above the booth said 3:55. I walked past it and out the door. Then I turned right.

Mobs of people were rushing by in the bright sunlight. Someone pushed past me

with a blaring radio. I walked along, trying to look confident, but when I got to the first corner, the sign said *Vanderbilt* Avenue, instead of Madison! Holding my breath, I crossed it and went on. The next corner looked like Madison, and it was. I turned onto it, practically running. I could see that the numbers were going in the right direction. Suddenly, at the end of the second block, I recognized the Zigmunds' building. What a relief!

The clock in the lobby said 4:05. Frantically, I ran into the first open elevator, but when the door closed and I looked for the 16 button, there wasn't one. What *was* this?

A man was watching me. "This car doesn't go past fourteen," he said. "If you want to go higher than that, you have to go back down and take one of the elevators across the hall."

So then I had to ride all the way back down, wait for the right elevator to come, and go back up in it. Finally, we got to the sixteenth floor. The door opened and I stumbled out, practically shaking with confusion.

The woman behind the desk looked up crossly as I opened the Zigmunds' door.

"You're Larry Pryor, right? You're late. Everyone else has gone off in the van." She opened a drawer and took out some money. "It's a red van. They're in the Sheep Meadow, in Central Park. You'll have to taxi over there and find them."

I stood there uncertainly. How would I do that?

"Hurry up now," she said, turning back to her work. "Everyone's waiting."

8

Action, Camera...

I didn't even know how to make a taxi stop for me. But when I ran out of the building and waved my arm at the first one I saw, it pulled right over.

"Central Park," I told the driver. "The Sheep Meadow." I sat on the edge of the seat, waiting for him to ask me where *that* was, but he didn't. He just flicked down the fare meter and started off.

"Nice day, right?" he asked, zooming up the street.

"Yeah." I was glad he didn't act surprised that I was by myself. Maybe New York City kids ride alone in cabs all the time.

We went through a whole row of green lights, swerving around cars and trucks.

"Get you there in no time," the driver said.

I sat back and watched the streets go by. It was good he knew how to get there.

"What part of the Sheep Meadow you want?" he asked, making a sudden turn. I could see some trees up ahead.

"I don't know," I said, feeling dumb. "See, I'm just meeting some people there— this television crew."

"That right?" The driver turned halfway around, still zooming in and out of traffic. "This cab you're in was on a TV show once," he said proudly. "Just the rear door, with some actor standing next to it, was all you could see when they showed it. But still—"

Suddenly, we crossed an avenue and drove right into a park. I hoped it was Central Park. There wasn't any sign. I stared out of the window, looking for the van. What if it wasn't there? But then the driver slowed down and I saw this big open field. That must be the Sheep Meadow! Then, I saw it—a red van, nearly as big as a bus.

"Hey, there they are!" I yelled.

The van was parked on the grass. Some

men were pushing cameras out of it. A
bunch of people were standing nearby. I saw
Suzanne! She was wearing her regular
clothes.

Quickly I looked at the meter, pulled out
my money, and gave the driver the four
dollars it said. I added another dollar because I know you're supposed to tip. Then I
wondered if I'd tipped too much. But the

driver didn't seem to mind. "Have a nice day, now," he said, pocketing the money.

"Thanks," I said, climbing out. I felt sort of pleased with myself for the way I'd managed the whole trip.

"Thank *you!*" the driver called through the window. "See you on TV!" Then he drove away.

At first, nobody even seemed to notice

me. But as I stood there, Suzanne looked up and waved. Then she came right over.

"Guess what, Larry?" she began, not acting the least bit surprised that I'd found the right place. "We get to wear these neat warm-up suits. They're blue with red stripes."

My hopes rose. "Aren't we going to wear underwear after all?"

"That comes later," Suzanne said. "But I saw it, Larry. It's not so bad. It's blue, too. It looks sort of like track shorts, with a top."

Before I could take that in, Mrs. Zigmund ran up.

"Larry!" she said, grabbing my arm. "Thank goodness you're here!" She seemed even more excited than usual. "Come along, both of you!" she cried, grabbing Suzanne's arm too, and pulling us toward the van. Her white beads bounced across her chest as she wobbled over the grass on her high heels. When we got to the open door, she gave us a little push. "Here they are!" she called into the van. "Here's Sis and Brother, ready for their makeup." Then she rushed off.

Makeup! I didn't know we'd have to wear *that*. I looked at Suzanne, but she was heading for a bench on the side of the van. I looked around. The whole place was full of microphones and boxes and equipment. People were talking loudly, waving combs and mirrors, unpacking boxes. There was a curtain across the back of the van. Maybe that was the dressing room. I wondered where they kept the underwear.

A red-haired woman suddenly bent over me. *"Hello!"* she said, in this actressy voice. "I bet I know who *you* are. With those cute red curls, you must be the Brother!"

Suzanne looked up. "His name's Larry," she said. "Larry, this is Darlene. She's our mother in the commercial."

"Hello," I said, trying not to act surprised by the way Darlene looked. I bet she was only about twenty years old. She was wearing this sort of sundress with hardly any top to it. Her face was stiff with tan-colored makeup, and she had false eyelashes about a mile long. She didn't look like any mother I ever saw. She certainly didn't look like *mine*.

Darlene patted her bangs. Her hair was a strange shade of red. Maybe it was dyed. "Isn't this fun?" she said gaily. "Being a little family?"

I nodded, to be polite, but Suzanne snickered.

"Who ever heard of a family with matching underwear?" she asked Darlene. "They'd have to be nuts. How would they sort their laundry?"

I laughed. Suzanne seemed much more friendly than the first time I saw her. I was glad she was there. I wouldn't have wanted to be Darlene's only child.

A small woman in jeans rushed into the van. "Darlene!" she said. "Get changed, pronto! They're going to be calling for you. Arnie!" She grabbed a man in a yellow shirt. "Why aren't these kids made up?"

"Coming!" Arnie put a box down beside Suzanne and began taking stuff out of it. "You first, Suzie," he said, dabbing powder onto her face. "Now, just a touch of lipstick." He held her face up, squinting at it. "And I'm going to give you some eyebrows.

Your own won't show up on film." He glanced over at me. "Yours won't, either," he said. "You new with the agency?"

"That's Larry," said Suzanne. "He's my brother, ha, ha." She grinned at me.

"Well, that's some Mom you two've got there, that's all I can say." Arnie winked toward the curtain where Darlene had gone to change. "I'm just waiting to see her pitch a ball. And Frank, too. I bet their only sport is watching football on TV!"

"Frank's the Dad," Suzanne explained to me. "He's outside." Her face looked funny with all the makeup.

"Okay, Suzie, get into your things," said the woman in jeans. "Just put the warm-up suit right over the underwear."

Suzanne made a face and stood up.

"Hi," the woman said to me. "You're Larry? I'm Liz Rodriguez, the producer of this crazy commercial." She picked up a big notebook and began leafing through it. "Let's just go over the script while Arnie makes you up."

I wondered how many pages she was

going to ask me to learn. How could I learn *anything* in all this confusion? A man in the front of the van was testing mikes. People kept shouting through the windows. Arnie was coming at me with a lipstick!

"Just a touch," he said, as I ducked away. "It won't even show on film."

It better not! The lipstick felt greasy on my mouth. Boy. If Robert saw me now, he'd really laugh. I shifted on the bench, thinking of Robert and all the kids back at practice. They seemed very far away.

"Hold still!" Arnie finished with my lips and started in on my eyebrows.

"The scene begins with Suzanne pitching to you," Liz said, studying her book. "Darlene's behind you, catching, and Frank's in the field. Now what we want you to do, Larry, is swing at the first ball. Swing and miss, okay?"

"Okay," I said, as Arnie stood back to look at my face.

"Then Darlene tosses the ball back to Suzanne," Liz went on. "Frank yells, 'Come on, Champ! You can do it!' Suzanne pitches again, and this time you hit one out over Frank's head and we see you and Suzanne and Darlene laughing as he runs after the ball." She looked up. "Think you can do that? I hear you're quite an athlete."

"Sure." She should have seen me catch that high fly in practice. I hoped I could do what she wanted now, with all those people watching and the cameras filming me. "What lines am I supposed to say?" I asked stiffly, through the lipstick. It tasted awful.

"You don't say a thing!" Liz smiled at me. "You're getting off easy your first time. Nobody says anything in this commercial, except Frank. And the announcer, of course. We'll record his voice-over later. He'll be telling about ChampWin products—the warm-up suits and the underwear."

"When does the underwear come in?" I had to know.

"Oh, don't worry about the underwear," Liz said easily. "It's pretty nice, actually. It looks sort of like gym clothes. I took a sample home to my son last week and he thought it was neat."

71

Yeah. But he didn't have to wear it on television.

Liz went right on. "The way we'll shoot this is, first, do some shots of all of you in the warm-up suits. Then, you'll take them off and we'll go through the whole scene in the underwear. That's all there is to it."

All? That was enough!

"Don't worry, Larry," Liz said. "You're gonna do fine."

"Ta-da!" Darlene came out of the curtain wearing her warm-up suit. You could tell right away she was an actress *pretending* to be an athlete. Suzanne came out next. She looked pretty good in hers.

Mrs. Zigmund's head poked into the van. "We're ready!" she said excitedly. "Mr. Corman's here to watch the filming." She looked at me. "Larry! Get yourself changed, fast!"

Then everyone piled out of the van, and I went behind the curtain. All my ChampWin clothes were hanging there. I took the underwear off its hanger and checked it out. It really wasn't too bad. The shorts did almost look like track shorts, and the top was just a regular sleeveless blue shirt. Both of them had red stripes, like the suits. If only the announcer didn't have to tell what it was, you *could* get by with it for gym clothes.

"Larry!" someone shouted into the van. "Larry Pryor!"

I had to get changed. Awkwardly, I pulled off my clothes, down to my own underpants, and pulled the blue ones on over them.

After all, nobody said not to do that. When I looked down, my legs were bare and white. I put on the shirt, which fit pretty well. Then I got into the warm-up suit. It felt nice and soft, the way new sweat clothes always do. Nervously, I checked myself out in the mirror. Not bad! If only I could wear the suit the whole time.

I made a face at the mirror. Then I pushed the curtain aside and walked to the door of the van.

This was it.

9

Shoot!

Everybody was gathered around a small baseball diamond that had been marked off on the grass. People were shoving cameras around and shouting at each other. I spotted Suzanne sitting on the third-base line and headed toward her.

The Zigmunds and Mr. Corman were watching everything from folding chairs. They all looked up as I passed.

"Don't you look adorable, Larry!" Mrs. Zigmund gushed.

"What did I tell you!" said Mr. Zigmund, nudging Mr. Corman. "A regular athlete type."

Embarrassed, I sat down next to Suzanne.

"Your suit looks good on you, Larry," she said matter-of-factly.

That made me feel better. "So does yours," I said.

Liz and Bud Slater were talking to a red-haired man in the same kind of suit.

"That's Frank," Suzanne said. "Our Dad."

Bud looked over and waved. "Hey, Larry. Good to see you."

We sat there for about fifteen minutes while everyone rushed around getting ready. Bud and Liz shouted out directions. People wearing earphones checked out mikes. A cameraman walked around holding a light meter over different spots. Everybody looked sort of tense.

"I didn't know it would take this long to get started," I said to Suzanne.

"Oh, it's always this way," she said. "Hurry up and wait." She leaned back on one elbow. "You know what I had to miss today, because of this? Rehearsal for my class play. *Oliver.* I'm just in the chorus, but still."

"You know what *I* had to miss?" I said

back. "My school team's first baseball practice." I hated to even think about it. I wondered if Coach Bryant had already assigned the positions. I wondered how many more practices I might have to miss.

"Anyway," Suzanne said then, "I heard they aren't going to do the other commercials for a while. Mr. Zigmund told Mom they might just use this one for a couple of months, before they do the rest."

"Hey, terrific!" That was the best news all day. "Then I won't have to miss any more practices. Or any games."

"And I won't miss any performances," Suzanne said. She pulled up a blade of grass and stuck it between her teeth. "Did you ever see *Oliver?*" she asked suddenly. "It's a neat show. If you wanted, I could probably get you a ticket, so you could come to it." She hesitated. "That is, if you wanted to."

"Sure," I said, surprised. Man! She was practically asking me for a date or something. No girl ever did that to me before. "You could come to one of my ball games," I told her casually. "You wouldn't even need a ticket." Boy. I wondered what the kids would say if a TV star like her came to watch our game.

"Okay," Suzanne said right away. "If I'm not working, I'd like to."

It was good I had Suzanne to talk to. It sort of took my mind off what was going to happen. She started telling me this stuff about commercials she'd been in. Like, she was in one for noodle soup where she had to say, "Oh, Mommy! It's noodlelicious!" She spent the whole day slurping up slimy cold noodles and saying "Oh, Mommy, it's noo-dlelicious!" until she practically threw up. Afterwards, she swore she'd never eat noo-dle soup again, but then the company sent her a whole free case of it! Her mother gave it away to the neighbors.

It's neat to hear inside stuff like that. I wished I could tell Robert about it, but how could I, without telling him *everything*?

Finally, Liz called, "Okay, actors—let's take up positions."

Suzanne and I looked at each other and stood up. A prop woman handed me a baseball bat and tossed a softball to Suzanne. She gave Frank and Darlene gloves. Then Liz and Bud showed us where to stand. My place was by a marked-off spot in front of Darlene. I swung my bat and got into a batter's crouch. Behind me, Darlene punched her glove and giggled.

"Okay," Bud said. "We're going to take shots of each of you, one at a time. Frank first."

They rolled a camera toward Frank and filmed him while he shouted, "Come on, Champ, you can do it!" about five times, and then they took him running after a ball about ten times. After that they filmed Suzanne winding up and pitching. Then they did Darlene catching, which took a long time because she missed so many throws. Last of all, they did me.

I had thought I'd feel nervous, standing there at bat with the cameras on me, but after the first couple of swings, I didn't. Suzanne stood out of camera range pitching to me. I swung and missed when Bud told me to, and when he said to hit one, I did. It made a good solid connection. The prop woman had to run way out past Frank to retrieve it. While we waited, I wiped my hands on my pants and kicked at the plate and swung my bat around.

"Great action, Larry!" Bud said suddenly, and I looked up and realized a camera had been on me all that time. I think I must have looked pretty professional.

Then Bud said, "All right. We're ready to run through the whole scene, in the under-wear. Take your suits off, folks."

Oh, boy.

I felt like a dope, standing by the tree and taking off my suit in front of everybody. I did the jacket first. Then I slowly took off the sweat pants. Beside me, Suzanne sort of giggled.

"I feel stupid," she said, tugging at her blue underpants.

"I know." I felt horribly bare. I glanced over at Frank and Darlene. They didn't seem at all self-conscious, although, if you ask me, they should have been. Frank looked sort of fat in the stomach, and you could see Darlene's shape making her shirt stick out. Some of the crew whistled at her, but she didn't seem to mind.

"Let's go, team!" she shouted, arranging her bangs as she ran to her place.

Frank jogged out to the field, and Suzanne said, "Well, here goes," and ran to the mound.

I tugged at my underpants, hesitating.

"Hey, whatcha doin? You making a movie or something?" somebody asked in a loud whisper behind me.

I wheeled around. A little boy, about five or six years old, was standing there staring at me.

"Nope," I said shortly. You'd think people would give you some privacy when you're working.

"Hey, what's that you got on, man?" he persisted. "Is that your *under*wear?" Then he laughed. I wondered where his mother was.

"Okay, Larry—position, please," Bud called.

Feeling the little boy's eyes following me,

I walked to the plate with as much dignity as I could and picked up my bat.

"Quiet, please!" Liz called out. "Everybody ready? Suzanne pitches, Larry swings and misses, Darlene throws the ball back, Frank yells, 'Come on, Champ, you can do it!' Suzanne pitches again, this time Larry hits it, and Frank runs after the ball. Got that?"

It was hard to concentrate with my whole

legs bare and that little kid watching. How could I go through with this? I swung my bat, trying to imagine how it would all look on TV. At least, I'd be smaller.

"Roll it!" Bud yelled. The cameras began to whirr. A man held up a slate that said CHAMPWIN FAMILY, TAKE 1. Bud pointed to Suzanne and she wound up and pitched.

Automatically, I jumped back. "Outside!" I called.

"Cut!" yelled Bud. "Larry, remember—you don't talk."

"Oh, yeah," I said, embarrassed. "Sorry."

The next time, the slate said TAKE 2. Suzanne pitched me a nice easy one that I could have walloped, but I swung and missed, the way I was supposed to.

"Oops, sorry!" Darlene squealed out behind me. I turned to look. She had dropped the ball and it was dribbling away from her.

"Cut!" said Bud. "Darlene—"

"Sorry!" Darlene said, punching her glove nervously.

On TAKE 3, I swung and missed and Darlene caught the pitch. But the camera caught Suzanne slapping at a mosquito on her arm.

"Cut!" Bud yelled again.

Man! I wondered if this would ever be over. Out of the corner of my eye, I saw the little kid sitting on the grass behind the sound man. He waved at me, giggling. I pretended I didn't notice.

The shooting went on and on. Just when the scene was almost perfect, some little thing would happen to mess it up, like Frank tripping over a branch when he ran after the ball, or Suzanne scratching her nose. Darlene kept dropping the ball, I started hitting pitches I was supposed to miss, and Suzanne's throws began to go wild. By this time, a whole crowd of regular people from the park had gathered. They stood behind the cameras, staring at us. I never felt so stupid in my whole life. If only I had some clothes on, I would show them how to slug one. But I bet even Reggie Jackson would make some mistakes if he had to hit in his underwear.

We were up to TAKE 14. I swung hard at the pitch I was supposed to hit, and missed.

"Sorry!" I yelled, disgusted.

"Hang in there, Larry," Bud called patiently. "Let's see if we can wrap it up on the next take, folks."

"Come on, gang!" Frank shouted, just as though he was psyching us up for a real game.

I took my stance.

Suzanne wound up and threw. I struck. Darlene caught the ball and threw it back. Frank called out his line. Suzanne pitched

again. This time I slugged it right past
Frank. He ran back after it and scooped it
up.

"Terrific!" Bud yelled. "Cut! Wrap it up!"

"That's it!" shouted Liz, slapping him on
the back.

We did it!

Darlene, Frank, and I ran up to Suzanne at the mound and stood there hugging each other like a real family. Bud and Liz came over to thank us. The crew began to push the cameras away. Over on the sidelines, a woman was shaking the little kid's shoulder. I heard him trying to explain: "It's a *movie!* I seen movie stars makin a real movie!"

Mr. Corman, with the Zigmunds after him, came to shake hands with each of us. "You're all champs," he said solemnly. "The company is proud of you."

Suzanne and I grinned at each other.

Mrs. Zigmund put her arms around us and said she was going to phone our parents and ask if we could stay in the city and go to a Chinese restaurant with the whole crew.

"Hey, neat!" I said.

"Scoot back to the van and change, kids," Liz said, smiling at us.

I jumped. I was so excited, I'd completely forgotten that I was only wearing underwear!

10

More Complications

I rode home on the train feeling exhausted but pretty pleased with myself. Look at all I'd done in just the one day. I'd found my way around the city, worked on a profession-al commercial, gone to Chinatown with the crew. (I'd eaten the whole meal with chop-sticks, too. Darlene showed me how. She's a real expert.) And on top of all that, a famous TV star was practically my girl friend!

Mom and Dad and Nancy were waiting for me at the Hazelton station. I got off the train feeling sort of like a hero. All the way home, my family kept asking questions and saying how wonderful I was to go to the city by myself. It was neat to tell them behind-the-scenes stuff about making commercials.

Mom and Dad started saying that I might become a star, and Nancy said she was really proud of me. (I think she was a little bit jealous, too, but she didn't let on.)

Anyway, I was so excited by my family's reaction that when Robert phoned and asked why I'd left practice that afternoon, I just couldn't hold it in any more.

"I went to New York," I said, as coolly as I could. "To be in a television commercial."

For a second, Robert didn't say a word. I guess I really surprised him.

"Are you *kidding?*" he croaked out then. "Are you really going to be on *TV?*"

Suddenly, I realized what I had let myself in for. But it was too late to take it back.

"How come you didn't *tell* me?" Robert was practically shouting. "What's the commercial for?"

"It's for this company called ChampWin Knitting Mills," I said, forcing myself to sound casual. My knees were shaking. "You know," I went on. "They make T-shirts and sweat suits. Stuff like that."

"Man!" Robert said. He was impressed, I

could tell. It would have been so neat, except for the underwear part. To distract him, I started describing the Zigmunds, and the way they discovered me. Then I told him about Suzanne, and how famous she was, and how she'd invited me to her school play.

"Is she going to be your girl friend or something?" Robert asked, sounding even more impressed.

"Probably." I felt sort of superior. I mean, old Stockton is nice, but all *she's* famous for is that she can wiggle her ears.

"Wow!" Robert was taking it all in. I braced myself for what he'd say next.

"Wait till I tell everybody!" he said excitedly. "They're never going to believe it!"

"Listen, Robert," I said carefully. "Don't say anything yet, okay?"

"How come?"

I thought fast. "See, they might not show the commercial for a long time. Maybe not ever. So why bring it up now?"

"Because it's *interesting!*" Robert said. "I

mean, I never knew anyone who was on TV before—"

"I'm *not* on," I said quickly. "That's the thing. I don't want people like Knudson to think I'm conceited, or making up some big story or something."

"Who cares what Knudson thinks?"

"*I* care!" I was practically desperate. "Robert, listen, promise me you won't say anything. Please!"

He must have thought I was crazy. But he's a true friend.

"Okay," he said reluctantly. "If you don't want me to, I won't."

"Thanks!" What a relief.

"But boy," he said. "Just wait! Wait till the commercial comes on. Everybody's going to go *wild* when they see you!"

"Yeah." If he only knew how right he was.

"Anyway," he said, turning serious. "You better tell Coach Bryant. So he knows why you had to cut out this afternoon."

Oh, man. I'd practically forgotten about that. It seemed like months ago. "Was the coach mad?" I asked nervously.

"Sort of," Robert said. "But I told him it must be an emergency or you wouldn't go off in such a rush."

"Thanks," I said quickly. Robert's a real friend. It made me feel rotten about not telling him the whole truth.

"That's okay." Robert cleared his throat. "Listen, Larry," he said. "The coach assigned positions today, after practice." He paused. "Knudson got first."

I *knew* it! "What did I get?" I asked, trying to sound casual. I hoped he'd say shortstop. Short's a good position. It's right in the center of things. In a way, it's more important than first.

Robert hesitated. "You're a substitute," he said finally. "See, the way it worked out was, Armbruiser got short, and—"

"That's okay," I interrupted. I didn't want to let on how disappointed I was. "Besides," I said, as sincerely as I could, "being on the team's the important thing. That's what counts."

"Yeah," Robert agreed quickly. "So, anyway, we have practice again tomorrow. You better explain to Coach Bryant before that."

"Sure." I hung up, feeling miserable. Substitute! It wasn't fair. I wished I could tell the coach the whole story, but I wasn't going to. Let him find out when everybody else did—when I came on TV in my underwear in front of the whole wide world and made a fool of myself. If only the Zigmunds had never discovered me that day! Now my whole life was ruined because of them.

The next two weeks went by in a blur. I tried not to think about the commercial, but I couldn't keep my mind off it. When were they going to show it? I kept waiting for the Zigmunds to call and worrying that Robert would blurt out my secret. It's awful to be on edge like that all the time. You can't concentrate on anything else.

And I had to concentrate on baseball. The Cardinals' first scheduled game was getting closer. I was determined to be in shape for it, even if I *was* only a substitute. What if Knudson broke a leg or something? I had to be ready to fill in.

Every day at practice, I played as hard as I

could. I wanted Coach Bryant to see I was trying my best. I wondered if he'd ever read one of those books where the substitute saves the game. I hoped so. What if Suzanne came all the way to Hazelton to see me play and he never even sent me in?

Sometimes I thought I would go crazy, with all the worries I had on my mind.

And then on Friday, the day before the first game, the worst worry of all came true.

They showed my commercial.

11

Exposed!

Ms. Sanford assigned a TV program on the Great Barrier Reef for homework. Robert came over to my house to watch it with me.

The program was pretty interesting, even though it was educational. Robert and I took notes all the way through. At the end of the show, Robert got up to switch channels so we wouldn't miss an early season game between the Mets and the Pirates.

Suddenly, before he touched the dial, a voice blared out:"ChampWin Knitting Mills presents—the underwear of champions!"

"Hey, look!" Robert yelled, pulling his hand back. "Larry, *look!*"

As I watched in horror, this kid on TV came up to the plate in a blue warm-up suit

95

that suddenly faded away to a picture of him standing there in his *underwear*.

It was me.

"Larry!" Robert started jumping around wildly. "Hey, Larry—that's *you!*"

"Move!" I yelled. "Move! Get out of the way!" I jumped up and shoved him aside so I could see.

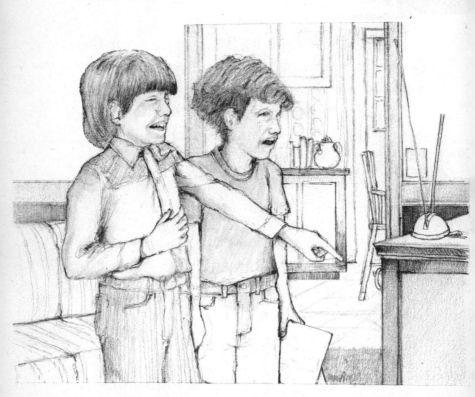

Music blared out of the set. "Get that ChampWin feeling!" the voice said loudly. And then the whole scene, that we'd gone through so many times, began to move across the screen.

"Looks great, feels great—great fit, for real family fitness!" the voice went on.

I stood there paralyzed. I couldn't look away. The little figures, dressed in underwear, seemed to be moving in slow motion. I kept staring at the one who was me.

The voice got even louder. "ChampWin underwear—the choice of champions!"

The music blared up again as the picture faded away. "Stay tuned—" a different voice began.

I grabbed hold of the dial and turned off the set. My knees felt weak.

"Oh, man!" Robert yelled, jumping up and down. "I don't believe it!" He punched my arm. "Underwear!" he shouted crazily. "Larry Pryor, the underwear champ!" He grabbed his stomach as though he was about to collapse. "Why didn't you *tell* me?" he demanded. Then he started howling again.

"Stop it!" I yelled. "Robert!"

But he didn't stop. "Oh, man!" he said, doubling up. "Boy, are you going to get kidded! Every kid in the *class* must have seen you! Wow, just wait till the game tomorrow!"

"Shut *up!*" I pushed him so hard he fell onto the couch. "Stop it, Robert!" I burst out furiously. "Why do you *think* I didn't tell you? Because I knew you'd act like this —like a little *kid!* What's wrong with you, anyway? How do you think *I* feel?" My mouth was dry. "How would you like every single kid in our class to see *you* in your underwear? How would you like them all to make fun of *you?* Man!" Angrily, I slumped down on the couch beside him.

Robert stopped laughing. He looked surprised. "I was just kidding, Larry," he said weakly. I could tell he was trying to get serious, but a little snort of laughter spurted out of him. "I mean—you know," he said, giggling helplessly. "It's just the *idea* of it. Of underwear." He sort of choked. "You were good, though," he said quickly, catch-

98

ing his breath. "No kidding, Larry. You looked neat."

Nancy burst in, with Mom and Dad behind her. "Larry! You were terrific!" She grabbed me and gave me a kiss. "I've been going crazy trying to find the commercial again for Mom and Dad, but I couldn't." Nancy has her own little TV set in her room.

"Oh, I wish I'd seen it!" Mom was all excited.

"Next time," said Dad. "You'll have lots of chances."

I could see Robert trying to straighten his face. "I guess I better go," he mumbled, not looking at me.

I knew what *that* meant. As soon as he got home, he'd be on the phone. He'd be laughing all night about the commercial with Stockton and everybody. I felt horrible thinking about it.

"You were good, Larry, no kidding," Robert said carefully, as though he was trying not to offend my parents. "Congratulations," he went on, backing toward the door. "See you tomorrow," he called, ducking out before he could break up again.

"Man!" I said angrily, when he had gone. "What a baby Robert is! He got all *excited,* just because of the underwear." I punched the couch cushion. "He made me feel stupid," I said, trying to keep my voice steady. "And just wait—every single kid in my class is going to be laughing at me at the game tomorrow. They're probably all laughing *now.*"

"Then *they're* stupid," said Nancy quickly, patting my shoulder. "It didn't really look like underwear anyway," she added comfortingly. "It was more like gym clothes." She sat down next to me. "Listen, Larry, I thought you were terrific. You looked like a professional. Honestly."

I knew she was just trying to cheer me up, but it helped a little. And Mom and Dad kept saying how proud of me they were.

"Anybody who teases you is just envious," Mom said. "Remember that, Larry."

"Yeah." The thing is, parents don't understand about teasing. They don't know how it feels. It feels *horrible.* Especially when you're nervous about something, the way I was about the game tomorrow. This was the worst possible thing that could have happened to me before a game.

Oh, man—the first game!

12

The Big Game

If there was any one thing I didn't want to do in my whole life, it was get up on Saturday and go to the game. But I had to go. If I stayed home, Coach Bryant would probably kick me off the team, and then I'd miss the whole season.

So I got up and went.

The breakfast Mom made me eat rumbled sickeningly in my stomach all the way to the field. I walked as slowly as I could. Instant replays of the commercial kept running through my head.

"Hey, Larry!" somebody yelled.

It was Stockton. "I saw you!" she said, running up. "I saw you on TV!"

Oh, man. "So?" I said, walking on.

"So that's pretty exciting!" said Stockton, sticking to me. "How come you never talked about it?"

"I don't know." What did she want, my whole life story, right before the first league game?

"I bet you were sort of embarrassed," she went on, laughing. "Being on TV in your underwear!"

"No, I wasn't," I lied, trying to keep calm. "I bet Robert and you were breaking up over it on the phone last night," I said, just to find out.

"We were not!" Stockton said right away. "I didn't even *talk* to Robert last night."

For a second, I felt better. Then Stockton went on. "Peggy Kearney called me after she saw you, and a couple of other kids, but that was all," she said matter-of-factly.

"Man!" I burst out. "The whole *school* must have been calling each other up!" It was even worse than I thought. How was I going to face everybody?

We had come to the edge of the field. It looked as though most of the team was already there. The kids were all huddled around the plate. They were probably talking about me. I would have liked to turn right around and go home, but it was too late. Knudson had already looked up.

"Hey, here he comes!" he yelled. "The *underwear* champ!"

Then they all started yelling. "Hey, Larry!" "Got your blue underpants on?" "I saw you, Pryor!" and stuff like that. They began crowding around me. "Underwear!" "The underwear champ!" they shouted.

"Shut up, will you?" I said furiously. "I don't want to even *talk* about it." I picked up a bat and swung it around to show I meant business.

Knudson had this stupid grin on his face, but he backed away.

"Are you guys going to stand here like dopes," I said, still swinging my bat, "or are you going to get out on the field and warm up?"

"Yeah, what is this?" Robert said, suddenly coming up behind me. "We have a game to play, remember? What are you trying to

104

do, ruin the team's morale? Let's get going. We have to warm up so we can *kill* those Jays!" He pulled at my sleeve. "Come on, Larry, let me toss some to you. I have to limber up."

"Sure," I said gratefully, heading for the bull pen with him.

"Don't pay any attention to Knudson," Robert said quietly. "Don't let him get to you. You have to stay cool. You're the only decent pinch hitter we've got."

I squatted down for his pitch. "It's not just Knudson," I said. "It's all of them. You'd think they never *heard* of underwear, the way they're acting."

"They'll get over it," Robert said, pitching a fast one.

"Yeah." I tossed the ball back. "In a million years, maybe." I was feeling a little bit better, talking to him. Anyway, *he* seemed to have gotten over it. I wondered if *I* ever would.

We warmed up like that for a while. All of a sudden the Blue Jays drove up in their bus and ran out onto the field. Coach Bryant got us together for a pep talk. Then the umpire yelled "Play ball!" and the game started.

Robert trotted out to the mound, but I had to go over and sit on the bench with Coach Bryant and the other two substitute players. Both of them were fourth graders. The one next to me punched me and started to make a remark, but he shut up fast when I glared at him. The Jays' first batter walked up to the plate. Robert wound up and the game began.

It was a terrible game. For four whole innings, nobody scored. Both teams made about a million errors. I sat there miserably on the bench as our team ran in from the field and ran back out again. Every now and then I yelled "Way to go, Robert!" or "All right, Cardinals!" but my heart wasn't in it. Meanwhile, the guys on the Jays' bench kept up a steady patter of insults, trying to psych our players out. It was disgusting. Just because they won the championship last year, they thought they were so great. But Robert and the other kids hung in there and the Jays didn't score.

Then, in the fifth inning, one of their batters slammed a double and the runner on base made it home. Their bench went wild, jumping up and down and slapping each other on the back. Coach Bryant groaned. I looked over at him, hoping he would think of sending me in when the Cardinals came up to bat, but he didn't say anything.

The game dragged on. I was too miserable to concentrate on it. I should have been analyzing Robert's delivery so I could help him practice later, but I couldn't focus my mind on it. All I could think of was the commercial and the way the kids had laughed at me. I felt stupid. And this was only the beginning. When I went to school on Monday, *everybody* would kid me. Even the first graders! I wondered if Suzanne's friends were kidding her. I wished I could just go home and call her up. She was the only person who would know how I felt. Anyway, it was pointless to just keep sitting there on the bench. I might as *well* be at home. What good was I doing? The coach was never going to send me in.

The game was practically over, anyway. Somehow, without my noticing, we had got to the top of the seventh, and our league just plays seven-inning games. Dully, I watched Robert strike out the Jays' first batter. The second batter up popped one out to left field, but the player after her got a base hit. The other two kids on the bench groaned, and groaned again when the runner stole second on a wild pitch. Now there were two outs, a runner on second, and the Jays' strongest batter walking up to the plate. On the first pitch he lined a hard one into right field. The runner on base rounded third and made it home, while the batter pulled up safe at first. Robert struck the next man out with three great pitches, but the damage had already been done—the Jays were ahead 2–0!

Our team dragged in from the field and flopped onto the bench. It was pretty obvious that we were going to lose the game.

But Coach Bryant wouldn't give up. "We can do it," he said encouragingly. "Never say die. Let's give it all we've got."

Everybody slapped each other on the back in a hopeless kind of way and Armbruster went up to the plate.

On the very first pitch, she slammed out a double!

"Way to go, Armbruiser!" everyone yelled, jumping up. I yelled, too, suddenly feeling hopeful for the first time that day. Armbruiser took a long lead off the base, ready to run. She looked serious.

Wyatt was up next. He's not that great a hitter, but after one strike and one ball he sent a solid drive down the third-base line and beat out the throw to first. Meanwhile, Armbruiser slid into third, safe. No outs, and the tying run on base!

I jumped up, cheering with the rest of the team. We might do it after all! Then I realized that Robert was the next batter. Robert's not the kind of pitcher who's also a good hitter. His batting average is not that great. He stood up and glanced over at Coach Bryant, with a grim look on his face.

"Pryor!" The coach leaned over and tapped my shoulder. "Get in there and show what you can do!"

All *right!* I jumped off the bench and headed for the plate. Stockton ran over with a bat. "Wham it, Pryor!" she said, giving it to me. "Do it the way you did on TV!"

Why did she have to say *that?* Swinging the bat in one hand, I came up to the plate, trying to get hold of myself. I had to get a hit—I *had* to!

Behind me, kids on the bench were yelling. "Slam it, Pryor!"

I took up my stance, wiped my hand on my pants leg and gripped the bat hard, trying not to think of anything except the ball that was going to come at me. The Jays' pitcher wound up.

"*Strike,* Shorty!" someone yelled from their bench.

Furiously, I swung at the pitch, and missed.

"Strike one!" the umpire yelled.

"Come on, Larry!" shouted Robert, as I waited out the next pitch.

It came at me suddenly, fast and inside. Before I could stop myself, I swung.

"Strike two!" called the umpire.

The Jays' bench hooted in triumph.

Tensely, I crouched into position, holding my bat tight. This was the last chance to show what I could do. Now or never. Out of the corner of my eye I saw some guy jump up from the Jays' bench and point at me.

The Jays' pitcher glanced around the infield and began to wind up. I watched his arm go over his head in what seemed like slow motion. I squinted at him tensely, trying to concentrate on the ball.

A yell came from the Jays' bench.

"Look! It's the *underwear* champ!"

The Jays were jumping around crazily. "Underwear!" "It's him—the underwear champ!"

The pitcher let go.

Throbbing with rage, I stood still, sizing up the ball as it floated slowly toward me. I braced myself, swung, and connected with a sudden tremendous crack. A roar went up behind me as the ball whizzed past the shortstop and sailed on toward the outfield. For an instant I stood frozen to the ground, so mad I could hardly move.

"*Go*, Pryor!"

Then I hurled down my bat and ran like a wild man, heading furiously for first. The cheers rose up as I rounded first without stopping and shot on toward second base. I'd show them! I touched second and raced on, with my heart pounding, dodging past the third baseman, touching base, and

starting for home. *Hey!* I was going to make it! I could see the whole team waiting for me. Gasping for breath, I put on one last spurt of speed and crossed the plate. I slapped Robert's hand and fell onto Wyatt and Armbruster, exhausted.

"Yea, *Pryor!*" The whole team jumped around me, thumping my back. "Yea, Champ!"

I stood there in a daze, taking it all in. I *was* a champ! I'd scored the winning run!

13

The Champ!

A few weeks later, a bunch of us were hanging around after practice, watching Robert work on his new floater pitch with Wyatt. He was going to use it in the next big game, a return engagement with the Jays. We were hoping to slaughter them. This time I was going to start off at first base. Knudson said I could, because Suzanne was coming to the game. That was pretty nice of him. He probably would have liked to show off for her himself.

"Hey, Champ," Armbruster said, pulling at my sleeve. Everybody calls me Champ these days. I don't mind. It's a good nickname. "Did you know your commercial was on about five different times last night?"

"Yeah, I saw it on the news," Halloran said.

"I didn't see it," I said. "I didn't watch television last night."

It was funny how my friends kept looking for the ChampWin commercial, just to see me in it. By now, they all must have known it by heart. Nobody made a big thing about the underwear any more. I guess when you've seen something like that so many times, it doesn't upset you that much. At least, that's how it was with me. At first, even after the Jays' game, I was embarrassed each time the commercial came on the screen. But after a while it just seemed ordinary.

Still, I have to admit it was sort of exciting when people acted as though I was famous. A few kids in the lower grades even asked me for my autograph! And kids in my class were always asking about inside stuff, like how they do fade-outs and sound effects. For a class project, I gave a report about making the second commercial.

There's no underwear in the new one.

Mr. Corman wants to get ChampWin into tennis clothes, so we all wear these neat white shorts and shirts. The commercial shows us playing doubles—me and Darlene against Frank and Suzanne. Darlene turned out to be practically a pro! In the script, she's supposed to keep missing shots, and we had to do about twenty-five takes before she managed to look bad enough.

"Hey, guys!" Robert yelled from the field. "Wanna have a quick batting practice?"

"Sure." Stockton grabbed a bat and ran to the plate.

Suddenly, I remembered. "What *time* is it?" I shouted.

Halloran looked at his watch. "Ten after four."

"Oh, man!" I said, panicked. "I've gotta go. I'm supposed to catch the four-twenty train to the city. Robert," I yelled, "I have to go! I have an appointment with the dentist."

"You just *went* to the dentist," he yelled back automatically, but I was already half-way across the field. Mom would kill me if I missed my check-up. I promised her I wouldn't forget. I sprinted all the way down Erie Street without stopping to catch my breath. I made it to the station just as the train was coming in. I dashed up the steps and ducked into the first car.

"Hi, there, Larry," the conductor said as I fell into a seat, panting. "Going to work again?" He knows me pretty well by now.

"Nope," I said. "To the dentist, this time."

I leaned back against the seat, catching my breath, as the train pulled out of the station. A minute later, we were passing the field. I leaned forward to look out the window. I could see the kids out there, jumping around. They looked good.

"Way to go, guys," I told them under my breath. Then I settled back to enjoy the ride.